MAY   2017

Lilly and Fin

A Mermaid's Tale

DISCOVER ALL OF CORNELIA FUNKE'S
ADVENTURES FOR YOUNG READERS!

Emma and the Blue Genie

The Pirate Pig

Ruffleclaw

Lilly and Fin: A Mermaid's Tale

Lilly and Fin

A Mermaid's Tale

CORNELIA FUNKE

ILLUSTRATED BY THE AUTHOR

TRANSLATED BY OLIVER LATSCH

RANDOM HOUSE 🏠 NEW YORK

Text and interior illustrations copyright © 2004 by Cornelia Funke
Translation copyright © 2017 by Oliver Latsch
Cover art copyright © 2017 by Vivienne To

All rights reserved. Published in the United States by Random House Children's Books, a division of Penguin Random House LLC, New York. Originally published as *Lilli und Flosse* by Dressler Verlag GmbH, Hamburg, in 2004.

Random House and the colophon are registered trademarks of Penguin Random House LLC.

Visit us on the Web!
randomhousekids.com

Educators and librarians, for a variety of teaching tools, visit us at
RHTeachersLibrarians.com

Library of Congress Cataloging-in-Publication Data is available upon request.
ISBN 978-1-5247-0101-7 (trade) — ISBN 978-1-5247-0102-4 (lib. bdg.) —
ISBN 978-1-5247-0103-1 (ebook)

MANUFACTURED IN CHINA

10 9 8 7 6 5 4 3 2 1

First American Edition

This book has been officially leveled by using the
F&P Text Level Gradient™ Leveling System.

Once upon a not too long time ago, there was a couple named Snorkel.

Mr. and Mrs. Snorkel were very rich. Quite unbelievably rich.

They owned a factory for licorice, and a factory for matches, and a lot of oil rigs. And a bank. And a zoo. And their own TV station. And there were thousands of other things they didn't even remember they owned.

You're probably thinking, *Wow! What did they do with all that money? Did they spend it on their kids?*

No. The Snorkels didn't even have kids.

But they had a hobby. A very expensive hobby. An aquarium.

Not just any aquarium. No! It was the biggest aquarium on earth, and it was stuffed to the brim with fish, crabs, sea serpents, and countless other

underwater creatures. And the Snorkels had caught every single one themselves.

Even though some of the creatures ended up being eaten by others, the aquarium still became so crowded that the smaller animals had to be moved into jam jars, and those jam jars ended up all over the Snorkels' house—on the stairs, on the bookshelves, on the breakfast table, and even in the refrigerator. (Those were the fish from the North Pole.)

And the Snorkels kept going hunting, and

they kept bringing back new creatures for their aquarium.

But there was one kind of sea creature they'd been hunting for years in vain. Their collection was still missing a genuine rainbow-scaled, green-skinned, fluorescent mermaid.

Mrs. Snorkel could barely think of anything else. And Mr. Snorkel was obsessed about this, too. They searched the seven seas with their lightning-fast submarine, the *Sea Devil*, and kept bringing back countless new creatures, but the mermaids eluded them.

Mr. Snorkel had even hired dozens of underwater detectives, but they couldn't find any mermaids, either.

The Snorkels were desperate. So desperate that Mrs. Snorkel had chewed the sea-green nail polish off her fingernails, and Mr. Snorkel had a stomach ulcer. Until one fine day . . . and with that day, our story begins. . . .

On that beautiful morning—I think it was the first of July—the doorbell rang at Villa Snorkel. A few moments later, the maid led a tall, thin man into the dining room. That was because Mr. and Mrs. Snorkel were just having their breakfast.

"Mr. Ignatius Harkenear!" the maid announced.

"The most famous underwater detective in the world!" Mr. Harkenear added, taking a deep bow.

Mr. Snorkel almost scalded himself with his hot coffee, and Mrs. Snorkel dropped her spoon into the marmalade.

"Oh, does that mean you have . . . ?" she cried.

"Yes, indeed, I have," Mr. Harkenear answered triumphantly. "I found mermaids."

"Where?" the Snorkels shouted simultan-
eously.

The detective went to the giant map of the
world hanging on the wall and put his finger on
a particular spot.

Where that spot was is top secret, of course.

"Here!" Mr. Harkenear said. "Right here
is the city of the mermaids. Very well hidden,
I have to say. But not well enough for the best
underwater detective in the world!" Ignatius
Harkenear showed them his most satisfied shark
grin.

"Fabulous!" Mr. Snorkel cried out. "We're leaving at once. Harkenear, you're coming with us."

"I'm always ready," the detective said, kissing Mrs. Snorkel's hand.

In no time at all, the Snorkels' servants packed the *Sea Devil* with everything one might need for hunting mermaids. The enormous submarine was moored in the basement, in a water basin that was as large as a football field. From there it could go through an underwater tunnel straight to the ocean.

Mr. Snorkel personally oiled the gripper arm with the pincers, which were big enough to grab a small whale.

After everything, absolutely everything, had been stowed on board, Mr. and Mrs. Snorkel climbed into their "Snorkel Special" diving suits. Then the submarine's hatch closed itself automatically with a loud bang, and the *Sea Devil,* gurgling and blubbering, sank into the water.

The hunt for mermaids was on!

Deep, deep down, at the bottom of a huge coral reef, was the city of the mermaids. This was no normal city. It had no houses or huts like humans would build. No, this city was made up of ships—ships that had been shipwrecked on the big reef and had sunk to the seafloor. It was in the bellies of all these ships that the mermaids lived.

Not a single ray of sunlight had ever reached this deep.

Now you're probably thinking, *Oh dear! It must have been pitch dark down there!* But it wasn't, because swimming in and around all these ships were glowing fish of all sizes that lit up the water day and night. Many mermaid families even kept their own glowing fish as pets—pet lamps, you might say.

For hundreds of years, the mermaids had

lived in these sunken ships. In the past, the mermaids used to swim up to the surface quite often, but at some point, there got to be too much traffic. Mermaid parents began forbidding their children to swim up there.

Even the smallest mermaids heard stories about the dangerous and terrible fishing nets and ship propellers—and the terrifyingly ugly Two-Legs who had invented all these awful things. Sometimes mermaid teachers took the older children up for a field trip so they could see that the grown-ups hadn't just been trying to scare them.

The very smallest of the mermaid children, however . . . well, they didn't really believe all those horror stories of Two-Legs and nets and propellers.

Nothing but scary stories, just like the tale of the giant kraken who lived in a cave and only came out to eat naughty mermaid children.

Some of the really naughty merpups sometimes even left the city. They sneaked past the

guards who kept an eye out for herds of sharks, gangs of moray eels, and other dangers. The merpups loved to go where the ocean was at its darkest. They played hide-and-seek or catch and only swam back home when they got really, really tired. Their parents would have gone crazy with worry if they'd known where their kids were.

This happened every day. But they had no idea. The mermaid parents also had no idea that a Two-Leg named Ignatius Harkenear had discovered their city. And they would never have guessed that a lightning-fast submarine called the *Sea Devil* was on its way to their city to catch one of them and put him or her into an over-crowded aquarium. After all, how could they?

Today they know, but back then all mer-maids believed that Two-Legs could only drive their ships up on the surface of the sea. None of the mermaid teachers taught their mermaid pupils that the Two-Legs had invented machines that could also go *under* the water.

They didn't know.

And that was bad. Very bad. Really bad.

Though it was, of course, quite handy for the Snorkels.

4

"How much farther is it, Harkenear?" Mr. Snorkel asked impatiently. He'd been standing all day by a large porthole of the *Sea Devil,* staring out at the green water, but he'd seen no sign of mermaids.

"Nothing but a bunch of stupid sea horses!" Mrs. Snorkel muttered as she chewed on her fingernails. "We've got at least twenty jam jars full of those."

"Patience!" Mr. Harkenear answered. "Not far now. Can you see that big coral reef there?"

"Yes, yes," Mr. Snorkel growled. "And? I've seen hundreds of those. Where are those mermaids, darn it?"

Ignatius Harkenear made a sour face. "Their city is right behind that reef. There's really no reason to get impatient."

"You keep talking about some city, Harkenear. I still don't believe it!" Mr. Snorkel barked.

"Who ever heard of fish living in a city?" Mrs. Snorkel chimed in.

"Mermaids are not fish!" Mr. Harkenear corrected them.

"Well, but very much like fish," Mrs. Snorkel replied angrily.

The detective shot her an insulted look. "Please stop the submarine as soon as we've circled that reef," he said. "The mermaids have posted guards around their city."

The Snorkels exchanged a glance and shook their heads.

"Guards . . . right!" Mr. Snorkel muttered.

He steered the submarine around the reef and stopped. The *Sea Devil* floated among the corals like a giant predatory fish. Beneath it lay the city of the mermaids. "But that's nothing more than a miserable ship graveyard!" Mr. Snorkel burst out angrily.

Then he fell very, very silent.

"There they are!" Mrs. Snorkel whispered, smooshing her big nose against a porthole.

Harkenear nearly burst with pride. "What did I tell you?" he asked. "Nobody has ever been able to find them, but I, Ignatius Harkenear, found them!"

"And I, Herman Snorkel, am going to catch one!" Mr. Snorkel announced.

His wife frowned. "Herman," she said. "Herman, look! There really are guards. There! In those crow's nests."

"Hmm!" her husband said, now also squeezing his nose against the porthole. "You're right! How annoying."

"And there's so many of them!" Mrs. Snorkel sounded quite worried. "How are we going to catch one without all those others becoming a problem?"

"Don't worry!" Mr. Harkenear said. "Absolutely no problem. We'll just catch ourselves a merpup."

"And what, I beg you, is a merpup?" Mr. Snorkel asked.

"A mermaid child. I have noticed there are

always some of them hanging around outside the city. One quick snatch with the *Sea Devil*'s claws and you got yourself a mermaid. It'll be a small one, but it'll last longer . . . ha-ha-ha!"

Ignatius Harkenear nearly choked laughing at his own wittiness.

"Perfect!" Mrs. Snorkel exclaimed, clapping her hands. "Then we'll keep our little merpup with our baby squid and boxfish—they'll look *darling* together!"

"Absolutely!" Mr. Snorkel nodded happily. "That is a fabulous idea, Harkenear. Let's get to it. I'll steer the sub behind those rocks there, and then we just wait for one of those merpups to swim past."

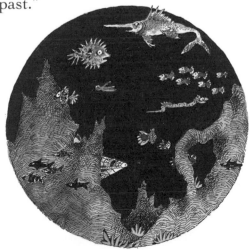

5

Most merpups are quite sassy, and smart, and not scared of anything, especially when they're small. And the sassiest, smartest, and bravest merpup was named Lilly.

She was eight years old and just about as big as your arm is long. Lilly had many friends, but her very best friend was Fin.

Fin was just one month older than Lilly, and two inches taller, and nearly as smart as she was. He had blue hair, and Lilly really liked him a lot.

Together they played almost every day, out in the wide ocean. And together they had discovered a cave behind a few big rocks, where they hid their treasure and played grown-ups.

The cave was absolutely one hundred percent secret, and it was the most beautifully gloomy cave in the whole wide ocean.

Whenever Lilly and Fin wanted to play in

their cave, Lilly would tell her parents that she was going to Fin's, and Fin told his parents that he was going to Lilly's. It always worked.

That day, as the Snorkels were maneuvering their submarine into hiding, Lilly and Fin were on their way to their cave. And why wouldn't they be?

They had absolutely no idea of the horrible thing floating out there.

Merpups can smell a shark or a moray eel from at least a thousand fin flaps away. But a submarine? How should Lilly and Fin be on the lookout for something they didn't even know existed? And they didn't believe in Two-Legs anyway, or giant kraken.

On that momentous day, Lilly's father had baked his delicious conch cookies and had packed a huge batch of them into Lilly's large seaweed bag. "There you go. Now you can have a nice picnic!" her father had said, adding a bottle of kelp juice to the bag as well.

Lilly gave him a big kiss on his big green

nose. "I'm going to Fin's," she said. "We're going to play treasure hunt. But I'll be back for dinner, okay?"

"Ah, treasure hunt. I used to play that myself!" her father answered. He lay down on his hammock to recover from all the cookie baking.

"I'll take Lamps with me," said Lilly. Lamps was one of the lantern fish they kept to light their home.

"Fine!" her father mumbled sleepily.

Lilly often took Lamps on her expeditions, as a sort of flashlight. And the little lantern fish liked going along. After all, just lighting up an

old captain's cabin day and night was not very exciting.

Lilly put Lamps on his leash (a real gold chain she had found in an uninhabited wreck). Then she slung the seaweed bag over her shoulder and swam out.

As usual, Lilly and Fin met in the wreck of a big old clipper right on the edge of the city.

Fin was already waiting on the deck when Lilly arrived.

"I brought cookies!" Lilly called as she paddled toward him. "And kelp juice!"

"Great!" Fin patted Lamps. "Listen, how

about we play here for a change?"

"Why?" Lilly's ears started to twitch. They always did that when she was getting annoyed.

"Because my scales are itching like crazy," Fin muttered. "And that means bad luck."

"Oh, you and your itchy scales!" Lilly swatted her tail angrily at him. "Nonsense! You probably ate too many fish eggs again, that's all."

"Really?" Fin frowned angrily. "Last time my scales itched, the morays nearly got us. And you didn't want to believe me back then, either."

"That's because I had a cold and couldn't smell them."

"And the time before that? You nearly got bitten by that nasty skate!"

"Puh! Just bad luck!" Lilly shrugged. "Come on, now. We'll be extra careful. I really want to swim to the cave. And if you're that scared, then I'll swim without you. And I'll eat all the cookies myself."

"That's mean!" Fin muttered, scratching his scales.

"Right. See ya!" Lilly turned around and swam away.

"Hey, wait!" Fin called. He slid off the deck. "I'm coming."

"You'll see. Nothing is going to happen," Lilly said when he caught up with her. But she was going to be very wrong about that. Their troubles began just beyond the city's boundary.

6

Have you ever heard of Neptune, the king of the seas?

No?

Well, you'd better pay attention, because you're about to meet him.

Lilly and Fin had no problem getting past the guards. They were, of course, mainly there to look out for sharks and other predators, not to keep an eye on adventurous merpups.

But Lilly and Fin had gotten just a few flaps of a tail fin away from the city's boundary when the sea around them began to tremble with mighty sighs and sobs. They exchanged a knowing look.

"Oh dear. You hear that?" Lilly asked, grasping Fin's arm.

"Of course. I'm not deaf." Fin groaned. "It's the fatso. I was right. Today will bring nothing

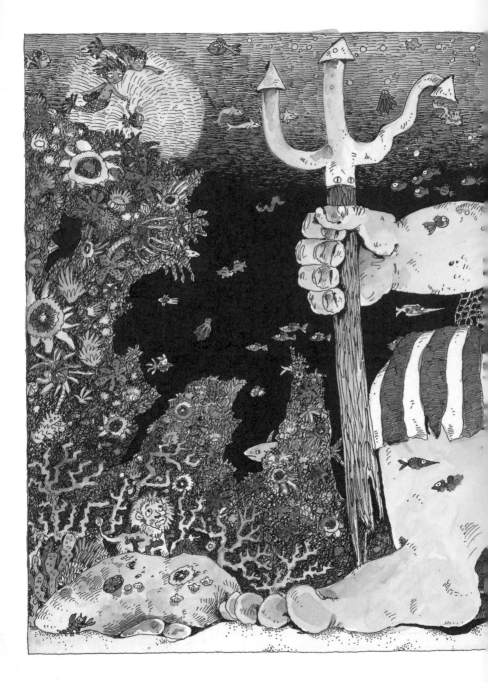

but trouble. Let's turn around. We can swim to the cave tomorrow."

"But I want to go today!" Lilly replied stubbornly. Her ears were flicking back and forth with excitement. "Maybe he won't notice us."

"Pfft!" Fin exclaimed. But he still swam after his little friend.

"He's down there!" Lilly whispered.

A big, fat merman was sitting on the bottom of the sea, crying bitterly. The tears were bubbling up his cheeks. (Sea creatures, of course, don't cry tears, but little bubbles of air.) The giant's nose was red and swollen. On his head sat a large crown, crusted all over with shells.

"Aaaaah!" he sobbed, pressing his big fingers in front of his face. "Oi weeeh!"

"Now or never!" Lilly whispered, and she dashed off.

That very moment the big man took the hands from his eyes. He sniveled and looked puzzled. And then he screamed, "Stop!"

Lilly and Fin swam a little faster, but they

were still too slow. The fat king grabbed them with his fingers and held them in front of his red eyes.

"Ah!" he roared. "Merpups. Little nasty merpups! Yuck! What are you doing here?"

"That's none of your business!" Lilly shouted. She was desperately trying to wiggle out of his big hand.

"Ha! Disgusting, impertinent little slitherers!" Neptune snorted. "I am the king, remember that!"

"You're not the king anymore," Fin retorted coldly. "You haven't been for centuries."

"Yes!" the fat man howled, shaking his fists,

and the merpups with them. "And that's why I am so sad." Tears started bubbling out of his red eyes again, and he let go of the merpups.

Lilly and Fin swam away as fast as they could. Neptune didn't even look after them.

"He crushed all my cookies!" Lilly muttered. "Just look."

"We'll eat the crumbs. So what?" Fin replied. "At least we got away quickly. The last time we spent an eternity in his pudgy fists."

"And poor Lamps," Lilly muttered on. "Just look at him. The shock almost turned out his light."

"If that's the worst that happens, I'll be happy," Fin growled. "My scales are itching like crazy. I think the real trouble is still ahead."

"Oh, stop it!" Lilly said impatiently. "You're already as crazy as the fat king. See? That's our cave. What could possibly happen now?"

"No idea," Fin replied. He looked around warily. But he didn't spot the metal nose poking out from behind a nearby rock.

7

"There!" Mrs. Snorkel called out. She was staring rapturously through the *Sea Devil*'s periscope. "There are two! Oh my goodness, they are adorable!"

"Let me see," Mr. Snorkel said, pushing his wife out of the way.

Lilly and Fin were clearly visible. Lamps had recovered from the shock of meeting the king of the oceans and was bathing the two merpups in his brightest light.

"Excellent!" Mr. Snorkel declared, grinning broadly. "Two of them. What do you think, my dear? Should we just take both?"

"Oh yes!" Mrs. Snorkel clapped her hands. "You know, we could put them in the entrance hall. In a pink fish tank! Then everybody will see them right away."

"May I?" Ignatius Harkenear cleared his

throat impatiently. "Do you think I could have a look?"

"Certainly!" said Mr. Snorkel, offering him the periscope. "You're the one who brought us here."

Flattered, the detective put his eyes to the ocular. "Nice specimens!" he declared expertly. "Quite a successful hunt indeed."

"Let's get the grappling arms ready," said Mr. Snorkel. "Those little wigglers will be swimming past here soon."

"No, Herman!" his wife called. "You always forget: the jars first!"

"Ah yes," Mr. Snorkel agreed. "Let's get to it!"

The Snorkels and Mr. Harkenear stepped onto a conveyor belt that brought them quickly and smoothly to the rear end of the *Sea Devil*. There they took an express elevator to the lower level.

"Heavens!" Mr. Harkenear breathed as they stepped off the elevator. "Quite something, isn't it?" Mr. Snorkel blushed with pride.

They were standing in a huge room lined with towering shelves that were filled with jars of every imaginable size and shape. Some were

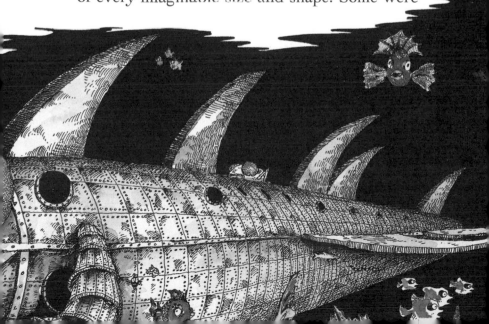

so small that they could only hold a single tadpole. Others were so big that they could comfortably accommodate a baby whale.

"I think those will be perfect," Mrs. Snorkel said, pointing at two jars that looked like large vases.

"Copy that!" Mr. Snorkel went to a large panel of buttons. "Number one-three-four," he said, pressing a button with his short finger.

Now it was time for Detective Harkenear to be even more amazed. A thin mechanical arm appeared from a hole in the wall and stretched itself up to shelf number 134. It grabbed one of the jars and carried it to a little round platform in the middle of the room. Then it did the same with the second jar.

"Phenomenal!" Ignatius Harkenear whispered. The Snorkels exchanged a proud wink.

The mechanical arm had now fetched a hose and was carefully filling both jars halfway with water. Not a single drop was spilled. Then the arm returned the hose to its place and gave a

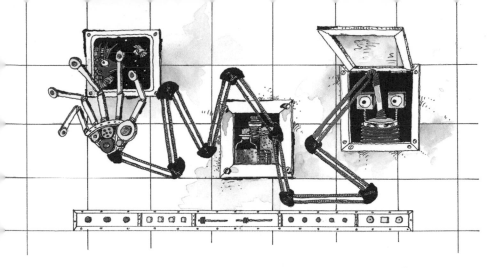

quick wave before disappearing back into the hole in the wall. Ignatius Harkenear was speechless.

"You see those pipes up there, Harkenear?" Mr. Snorkel asked. "They come straight down from the grappling arms. Works just like your everyday vacuum: the merpups will be sucked into these pipes, which will drop them into these jars. The arm will put lids on them, and we're done. What do you think?"

"Absolutely perfect!" the detective answered enthusiastically.

"My invention," Mr. Snorkel declared.

"Herman!" Mrs. Snorkel tugged her husband's sleeve. "We have to get back up front, or we'll lose these darling creatures after all."

"Copy that!" Mr. Snorkel quickly led them to the elevator.

Once back on the bridge, Mrs. Snorkel immediately headed to the periscope. "Hurry, Herman!" she called. "They are swimming right past us. Quickly!"

Mr. Snorkel hit about twenty buttons in very quick succession. The long grappling arms shot out from the sides of the submarine, their big claws snapping wide open.

"Did they see us?" Mr. Snorkel asked.

"No!" his wife answered.

"Excellent!" Mr. Snorkel grinned his widest grin—the one that showed all his yellow teeth. "Then we've got them."

And slowly, very slowly, the *Sea Devil* crept out of its hiding place.

8

"Lamps, what are you doing?" Lilly huffed. The little lantern fish was constantly circling her, wrapping his leash around her tail. He was flickering like an old lightbulb and bubbling excitedly.

"What's the matter with him?" Fin asked uneasily.

"No idea. Maybe he just wants a cookie." Lilly gave him some crumbs. "And now, shush!"

Lamps quickly swallowed the crumbs, but then he started darting around her again.

"We'll be there soon," Lilly said. "Then he can get off the leash."

Fin slowed down. "Do you hear that hum?" he asked, holding Lilly back by her arm.

"What hum?"

Fin looked around—and froze. And now Lilly saw it, too.

A huge silver something was drifting toward them. Its massive crablike pincers were snapping open and shut. The monster was bigger than anything Lilly had ever seen in her short life. Fin just stared at it. "Fin! Swim!" Lilly screamed.

But her friend still didn't move. His wide eyes were just staring at the terrible pincers, and before Lilly knew what was happening, one of them had sucked up her friend. It closed with a loud clang. And Fin was gone.

Sobbing, Lilly turned around and swam. She swam as fast as she could, but the humming came closer and closer. She could already feel the second pincer reaching out for her. Just then she spotted a little crevice in the rocks. It was pitch black and didn't look at all inviting.

Normally, a smart merpup such as Lilly would never have swum into a place like that. There could be morays hiding inside, poisonous sea serpents, and a thousand other hideous dangers. But right now that crevice was Lilly's only chance. She dashed into it with her last bit of strength. Behind her, the big monster crashed into the rock with a crunch.

Two large, bright eyes lit up, shooting out long, thin fingers of light that shot around in the dark, looking for the little mermaid.

It was the first time since the beginning of the world that light had entered that dark crevice, and all the creatures that lived there hid themselves in the cracks and crannies, squeezing their eyes shut against its painful brightness. This was good for Lilly, for it kept those creatures from biting or stinging her as she dashed along the crevice at high speed.

Her heart felt like it was about to explode. Her little tail was aching, and her eyes were bubbling big tears.

Suddenly the crevice got tighter, and then it took a sharp turn. The fingers of light from the monster could no longer follow her, and the merpup was surrounded by darkness. Thousands of eyes were staring at her. Lilly felt her way along the rock and then realized that the crevice ended in a huge cave.

What now? Lilly thought. Trembling, she shrank back, away from the darkness and all those eyes. But soon enough she could see the light fingers going all over the rocks.

Lilly was trapped. "So I can't go back. That much is certain!" she muttered. "I can't swim out the top—the monster would see me there as well. So all that's left is that big black hole there." Lilly's ears were twitching. "Or I wait here until the monster's gone."

But what about all those scary eyes? She slowly swam toward the pitch-black cave again and peered inside.

Suddenly something soft shot out of the cave, wrapped itself around her hip, and pulled her into the darkness.

9

And Fin?

Fin only came to after the giant pincer had snapped shut around him. He immediately started hammering against the walls, noticing to his surprise that they were cold and smooth. They felt nothing like the pincers of a crab or a lobster. They didn't feel like anything Fin had ever felt before.

This is a strange monster, he thought as he waited for it to stuff him into its mouth and swallow him. Instead, he felt something pulling at him. He tried to hold on, but there was nothing to hold on to, just cold, smooth walls.

He was being sucked toward a narrow tube.

Now I'm getting swallowed! Fin thought, and with that, he was already sliding headfirst into the tube. The little merpup shot like a cannonball down a long pipe. His head ached, and his

rainbow-colored scales felt very, very itchy.

Then, suddenly, there was a lot of light. Fin flew through the air, only to land with a loud splash in water again. It was the strangest kind of water he'd ever seen. It had no color whatsoever. And when Fin reached out with his hands, they quickly hit an invisible wall.

That wall was all around him. Fin could barely turn without hitting it with either his head or his tail.

And the place was bright. Terribly bright. The light hurt his eyes and blinded him.

Something dark came down from above and shut his see-through prison with a loud squeak.

Fin pressed against it with all his strength, but it didn't budge. Now he was truly trapped.

But where?

Where was he? What was he in?

So . . . I definitely haven't been eaten, the merpup thought. *This really doesn't look like a stomach. Or does it?* After all, he'd never actually been in a stomach.

But before Fin could form his next thought, he was already in for another shock. Three huge figures were approaching his prison. Fin couldn't see them properly, because his eyes just would not adjust to the horrible light. Blinking and squinting, all he could see was that they were coming closer.

As little as he could see, he did notice that the three creatures were absolutely hideous-looking. And they were walking on legs! Two-Legs! The thought shot through Fin's aching head. *Those are Two-Legs!*

The hideous faces were coming ever closer, until their big noses squished against the invisible walls of his prison.

Oh no, now I'm going to get eaten after all! Fin thought. And he squeezed his eyes shut.

10

"Goodness, how adorable!" Mrs. Snorkel called as she leaned closer to the jar with their new prisoner. "Herman, look! I think this is a mer-boy. Isn't he cute?"

"Indeed!" Mr. Snorkel had a satisfied grin on his face as he stared down at his trophy.

"That blue hair will go very well with the pink baby squid!" Mrs. Snorkel sighed happily. "Look, he's closing his eyes. He's probably shy. How cute!"

"I think this one's quite young," observed Ignatius Harkenear as he studied the prisoner with scientific interest.

"Oh, Herman, what a pity the other one got away," said Mrs. Snorkel. She was staring, mesmerized, at Fin's shimmering scales. "They would have gone so well together. We could have put them in the living room, right next to the television. I would have put little seashells into their tank and—"

"We'll get that other one," Mr. Snorkel interrupted his wife. "We'll simply wait by that crevice. Eventually she'll have to come out of there. And then we'll grab her."

"Definitely." Ignatius Harkenear nodded. "Hunger—or curiosity—will drive her out eventually, and then—snap! Ha-ha-ha!" The detective's entire body shook with laughter.

Mrs. Snorkel tapped against the glass, but Fin kept his eyes closed and didn't move. "You know, Herman," she said, "I don't think those little creatures are very smart."

"Definitely not." Mr. Snorkel smiled arrogantly. "Not much space for brains in those little heads."

"Yes," Mrs. Snorkel agreed. "But maybe they can still learn a few tricks?"

Fin opened his eyes and shot her a sinister look.

"Herman!" Mrs. Snorkel cried. "Look!

He's staring at me. But he doesn't seem very friendly."

Fin crossed his arms and stuck out his blue tongue at her.

"Oooh!" Mrs. Snorkel huffed. "Herman! That little fish is rude!"

"Maybe that's how mermaids say *hello*," Mr. Harkenear suggested. He eyed the prisoner skeptically.

Fin stuck his tongue out at him, too.

"There. See?" Harkenear pointed out. "It definitely means 'hello'!"

"Hmph!" Mr. Snorkel grunted, unconvinced. "Never mind. I say we go up front and catch the other mermaid."

Together they marched back to the elevator.

"I hope she doesn't take too long to come out," Mrs. Snorkel said. "I really do hate waiting."

11

Lilly wasn't feeling much better than Fin. The big, soft arm that had grabbed her was pulling her ever deeper into the dark cave. Lilly wriggled and cursed and pinched and bit, but none of that had any effect. The cave entrance had shrunk way into the distance, and Lilly was surrounded by nothing but the blackest darkness.

Suddenly the arm put her down and let go of her.

Lilly would have loved to swim off quickly, but where would she have gone? To her right, nothing but darkness.

To her left, nothing but darkness.

Behind, above, in front, not even the tiniest speck of light. Lilly had absolutely no idea which way the exit was. If only she had Lamps with her now. Where had he gone to anyway?

Then she suddenly heard a deep voice say, "Welcome!"

Two huge eyes lit up in the darkness. "I'm sorry it's so dark in here," the voice continued, "but my lantern fish are terribly lazy. Wake up, you sleepyheads! We have a visitor." Lilly heard murmurs and mutterings all around her. Then she saw lights shimmering and glittering. "About time!" her host said.

Now Lilly could see him — and she froze with fear.

Sitting in front of the mergirl was a fire-red octopus the size of a mountain. His arms were thicker than the biggest masts in the city of the mermaids. "I hope I didn't give you too much of a fright," he said, giving Lilly a friendly nudge with one of his arms. The poor mergirl's heart nearly stopped. "I just couldn't help myself, seeing you out there. I so rarely get any visitors."

"The giant kraken!" Lilly breathed. "He exists!"

"Oh, so you've heard of me?" the kraken asked, flattered.

"Of course!" Lilly mumbled. She didn't even dare look at the giant animal. "Do you really eat merpups?" she asked with a thin voice.

"Yuck! No!" the kraken called out. "Why would you think that?"

"My parents told me," Lilly answered.

"Complete nonsense!" The kraken angrily tangled up some of his arms. "I'm a vegetarian. Though I may have a couple of mussels on very special holidays."

"That's a relief!" Lilly said. "I thought I was going to be eaten as well."

"Why 'as well'?" the kraken asked. "Who else got eaten?"

"Fin!" Lilly whispered, and the tears again started bubbling up from her eyes.

"Who is Fin?" the kraken asked tenderly.

"My very best friend forever!" Lilly sobbed. "And it's my fault. He didn't even want to come, but I bullied him into it. And now the monster ate him."

"A monster. Really?" The kraken rocked his

head back and forth. "You'll have to explain that some more. With your permission, could I lift you up a bit? Otherwise I can hardly hear your little voice."

Lilly hesitated, but then she nodded. The kraken gently rolled up the tip of one of his arms and offered it to Lilly.

"Please, make yourself comfortable," he said.

Lilly sat down carefully on his arm, and the kraken slowly lifted her up until she was right in front of his giant eyes.

"Now, what kind of a monster was it?" he asked.

Lilly wiped the tears from her eyes. "A giant monster. Nearly as big as you."

"Nearly as big as me?" The kraken scratched his head. "I don't like the sound of that. Tell me more."

"It has huge glowing eyes," Lilly called, "and big beams of light coming out of them. They can follow you everywhere."

"Sounds hideous!" The kraken sighed. "Go on."

"It has pincers, like a crab's, just much bigger, and it tried to grab us with them. And then . . ." The little mergirl started sobbing again. "Then it ate Fin."

"Now, now!" The giant kraken gently rocked Lilly on his arm. "I really do not like the sound of that at all! In fact, it actually makes me quite angry. Who does that monster think it is? Hunting merpups right in front of my own home. The nerve! In all the hundreds of years I've been living here, nobody has ever dared do something like that." The kraken rolled his eyes angrily,

which looked quite scary. "What do you say? Should we go and have a look at that monster?" he asked.

"Well, I . . ." Lilly didn't know what to answer. Merpups are really extraordinarily brave, especially the small ones, but that day had been too much, even for Lilly.

"You don't have to be afraid," the giant kraken told her. "I'm sure I can handle that little monster of yours. I just thought you might want to watch."

Lilly thought of poor Fin and the terrible pincers. Then she nodded. "I'm coming."

"Great!" the giant kraken said, throwing Lilly up like a Ping-Pong ball. "I haven't had this much fun in centuries. That monster won't know what hit it."

12

The kraken's cave had many exits. One of them was high up between the rocks.

From there one had a first-class view of the crevice Lilly had fled into, and the *Sea Devil* hovering in front of it. "There it is!" the kraken whispered.

"Yes. That's the one," Lilly whispered back. "It's waiting for me to come out. Yuck!"

"It really is quite big," the kraken observed. "But not nearly as big as I am. I'll swim a little closer. Come."

They stopped behind another rock. "You've been telling me fibs!" the kraken growled.

"What? Why?" Lilly asked, surprised.

"That there isn't an animal at all. Or have you ever seen an animal made of metal? With screws and bolts and eyes made of glass?"

"No, but what else could it be, then?" Lilly was confused.

"That, you little pup, is a Two-Legs machine."

"What? So Two-Legs are also real?"

The kraken shot Lilly an angry look. "Of course! You really don't know much at all, do you?"

"I . . . I just thought they were a scary tale for merpups. Just like . . ." Lilly stopped, looking embarrassed.

"Just like the giant kraken." The kraken gave her a friendly nudge. "I get it."

"How do you know about the Two-Legs?" the mergirl asked.

The giant kraken rolled his eyes and started getting yellow spots all over his head. He always got those when he was embarrassed.

"When I was younger, I'd sometimes play with their boats. You know, shake them a little. I thought that was funny, until I realized that the Two-Legs didn't always survive falling into the water. Since then I just scare them a little every so often."

"Do they really eat merpups?" Lilly asked.

"No idea. Maybe. Why do you ask? Oh, because of your friend?"

Lilly nodded.

"You know," the kraken said, "maybe they just caught your friend so they can eat him later."

"But then we could still save him!" Lilly looked at the kraken, hope in her eyes.

"Not a problem!" the kraken replied. "Come on. Those Two-Legs aren't stupid. They built themselves quite a nice little machine there. But now it's time I gave it a bit of a shake."

13

Mr. Snorkel's eyes were red.

"I can't keep staring through this stupid thing!" he muttered, pushing the periscope aside.

"She'll be coming out any second!" Mrs. Snorkel said. "I can feel it."

"Humbug!" Mr. Snorkel growled. "You've been saying that for hours." Ignatius Harkenear was lying on the floor. He'd been asleep for a while now.

"We've caught giant sharks!" Mr. Snorkel ranted on. "And long sea serpents. But it has never taken this long. Blasted little slithers!"

"Herman! Something's coming!" Mrs. Snorkel suddenly called.

"Sure!" Mr. Snorkel kept pacing up and down.

"Herman! It's huge!" Mrs. Snorkel cried.

"Whatever!" Mr. Snorkel muttered. "We should just take that one merpup and call it a day. Let's go back home."

The answer came as a piercing shriek. Mrs. Snorkel had jumped back from the porthole and was now cowering behind a chair.

Someone was looking in through the thick glass, with eyes the size of an umbrella.

Mr. Snorkel began to tremble all over. "Harkenear!" he breathed. "What is that out there?"

But the detective was still snoring peacefully in his corner.

Suddenly the *Sea Devil* began to shake as though it was in the grips of a mighty storm. Mr. Snorkel, Mrs. Snorkel, and Mr. Harkenear were rolling around the floor like marbles. Ignatius Harkenear finally woke up. "What is going on?" he shouted.

"Out there!" Mr. Snorkel panted as he rolled under a table.

"What?" Mr. Harkenear shrieked as he rolled against the wall.

The giant eyes were still staring through the porthole, and they looked amused. For a brief moment, a little face also appeared in the glass, but nobody noticed that in all the commotion.

"Our beautiful submarine!" Mrs. Snorkel wailed. "Herman, do something! I'm already bruised all over."

"We have to get to the escape pod!" Mr. Snorkel huffed. He was trying to crawl away, with Mrs. Snorkel and Mr. Harkenear behind him on all fours.

The escape pod sat on top of the *Sea Devil* like an ugly wart. The only way in was up a narrow ladder. All three tried again and again to climb up, but the shaking and wobbling just wouldn't stop, and they kept dropping off the ladder like ripe fruit. When they finally all made it to the top, they had bruises everywhere.

"Seat belts!" Mr. Snorkel yelled.

The other two strapped themselves in with trembling fingers. "Herman, we forgot the mer-pup!" Mrs. Snorkel whined.

"Why don't you get him, then?" Mr. Snorkel barked at her.

"No! No!" Mrs. Snorkel whispered. "I think I'd rather not."

Mr. Snorkel pressed a shaky hand down on a huge red button.

The little rescue pod gave a jolt before screeching toward the surface at breakneck speed.

The three passengers cast one last glance back, and what they saw made their hair stand on end: their beautiful *Sea Devil* was being squeezed like an empty soda can by the giant arms of an enormous bright red kraken. And one of those red arms was just now reaching for their escape pod.

14

Fin was still sitting in his tiny prison when the giant kraken started shaking the *Sea Devil*.

The first jolt made the jar fall off its pedestal. It started rolling noisily back and forth on the floor.

It was horrible. Just horrible!

Hundreds of jars started rolling all over the big room. They smashed into the walls and into each other, and to Fin's huge surprise, some of them even shattered into thousands of tiny pieces. "Oh no!" he gasped. Out there was air, nothing but disgusting, deadly air. Not a drop of water anywhere. And his prison was rolling toward the wall again.

Fin squeezed his eyes shut. *This*, he thought, *is definitely the worst day of my life, and the way things are going, it's also going to be my last.*

Outside, Lilly was shouting, "What are you

doing?" She was swimming in front of the giant kraken's eyes.

"I'm just giving those Two-Legs a little shake!" the giant kraken howled with delight. "They really don't like that at all!"

"But what about Fin?" Lilly cried. "Fin probably doesn't like it, either. You're hurting him!"

"Nonsense!" the giant kraken boomed. This was way too much fun to just stop. "They'll come out soon. You'll see!" He began to hum to himself.

"Who's coming out?" Lilly asked.

"The Two-Legs, you dimwit!" And at that very moment, the rescue pod shot away from the *Sea Devil.*

"See?" The giant kraken triumphantly tucked the rather dented submarine under one arm and stretched another arm after the escapees. Soon the arm had wrapped itself around the pod, and the kraken leisurely started pulling it in.

"Want to have a look inside?" he asked Lilly. "Maybe your friend is in there."

Lilly peered through one of the portholes. "Yuck!" She shook herself. "They're disgusting. So pale. And one of them has funny eyes."

"Hmm." The kraken nodded. "There's also dark-skinned Two-Legs. They aren't quite so disgusting. Though they're all fairly yucky anyway."

"But Fin isn't in there," Lilly observed. She hung her head disappointedly.

"Well, he's probably still in that other thing." The kraken apologetically shrugged his many shoulders. He shook the capsule like a rattle. "What shall we do with the Two-Legs?"

"I don't know." Lilly suppressed a sob. "I don't care. I just want Fin back."

"Fine, I'll let them swim," the kraken said. "They're not good company, and they make very boring toys, and they definitely don't taste good. Off you go, then!"

He cast the capsule away. For a few moments, it just wove through the water like a drunken bug. Then it shot off toward the surface.

"Don't show yourselves around here again!" the kraken called after it, waving all his arms.

Lilly could only think of one thing: what had happened to Fin?

15

The kraken had stopped shaking the submarine, and Fin's jar was still intact.

It rolled across the glass splinters that now covered the entire floor, before stopping in a corner. Suddenly everything was still. Very still.

Exhausted, Fin closed his eyes and leaned against the cold glass. His heart was still beating like crazy. But just as it started to slow down a bit, something knocked against his invisible prison.

The Two-Legs are back, the merpup thought. *Well, I don't care.* Another knock.

And another. And one more.

"Nobody's home!" Fin grumbled.

He reluctantly opened one eye—and quickly shut it again.

Now I've gone completely mad, he thought. That had looked like a huge kraken arm.

His prison was lifted up. The jar rocked back and forth. Fin opened the other eye. It was a kraken arm. A huge bright red arm. And it was carrying him toward a broken porthole, through which he could see the friendly shimmer of the ocean.

Fin groaned and shut his eye again. *That's enough,* he thought. *If on top of everything else I'll now also get eaten by a giant kraken. . . .*

"Hey, Fin!" Lilly called. She kept knocking on the glass jar. "Open your eyes. Come on! It's me!"

But the merpup kept his eyes firmly squeezed shut.

"Can you open this?" Lilly asked the kraken.

"Sure." The giant kraken wrapped the tip of one of his arms around the lid and squeezed it gently. *Plop!* The jar opened. Green seawater rushed inside. Fin opened his eyes.

"Finally!" Lilly exclaimed, beaming at him. "Come out of there."

"No way!" Fin growled. He shot a very

worried glance at the giant kraken.

"You don't have to be scared of him," Lilly said. "He's a friend of mine."

"You've got some funny friends," Fin growled again. He stayed right where he was.

So the kraken just tipped the jar upside down and shook the merpup out. "There!" he said, tapping his tentacle against Fin's chest. "And now you can apologize for your bad manners, and you can thank me for rescuing you. Or I'll eat you after all!"

"Thanks. And sorry," Fin said quickly. He floated behind Lilly's back.

"You're welcome," the giant kraken answered. "The pleasure was all mine. Haven't had this much fun in a long time. And what do we do now?"

"Now we have to get home, and quickly!" Lilly answered. "If I'm not back for dinner, I'm going to be in big trouble."

"Not a problem!" the giant kraken boomed. He held out a tentacle to the two merpups. "I'll be your taxi!"

16

And so the giant kraken brought Lilly and Fin home. Not all the way home, for that would have caused too much alarm in the city of the mermaids. No, he dropped them just where the guards couldn't see them.

"Good-bye," he said. "I do hope you'll come and visit?"

"Sure!" Lilly promised, nudging her friend.

"Definitely," Fin muttered, though he still thought the kraken was too big.

They all waved at each other, and then the kraken disappeared between the rocks. Lilly and Fin turned around and swam back into the city.

"Next time my parents talk about the terrible giant kraken," Lilly said, "I'm probably going to laugh!"

"Well, I definitely won't laugh next time

someone talks about the Two-Legs," Fin muttered. "They're even worse than in all those stories."

They swam past the guards.

"What shall we do tomorrow?" Lilly asked.

"I'm going to sleep tomorrow," answered Fin.

"The whole day?"

"The whole day."

"Hmm."

For a while, they just swam silently next to each other.

"Fin?" Lilly finally asked.

"What?"

"I promise: I'll listen to you the next time your scales itch."

Fin shot her a wary look. "Promise?"

"On my honor!"

They had reached the shipwreck where Lilly lived with her parents. "So you'll be sleeping all day tomorrow?" Lilly asked again.

"Maybe not," Fin answered, grinning. "Might get a bit boring, don't you think?"

"Great! Then let's meet tomorrow. The usual place?"

Fin nodded.

Suddenly a small lantern fish came zooming toward them. "Lamps!" Lilly sighed with relief. "You found your way home."

"Hey, you coward!" said Fin.

"He doesn't feel guilty at all." Lilly observed.

"Oh well." Fin yawned. "See you tomorrow."

"See ya!" Lilly waved until Fin had disappeared behind the next wreck.

"I'm so glad the Two-Legs didn't eat him," she whispered to Lamps. "After all, he's my very best friend."

And then she and the little fish swam toward the brightly lit cabin where her parents were already waiting for her.

17

Do you want to know what happened to the Snorkels and Mr. Harkenear?

Well, their escape pod drifted across the ocean for over a week, until a huge, rusty freighter fished them out of the water.

Mr. Snorkel and Mr. Harkenear both had a beard and a black eye because they had spent all the time fighting over whose fault it was that their hunt had gone so completely wrong.

Mrs. Snorkel of course did not grow a beard, but she had red eyes from crying because she now didn't have a merpup to put with her pink baby kraken. And all three of them were seasick from the escape pod bobbing on the waves. And they still had their bruises from being shaken by a giant kraken.

They kept fighting even on board the

freighter, until its captain finally threatened to leave them on some deserted island. From then on, they just shot each other nasty looks and kept trying to trip each other up.

Mr. Snorkel kept muttering, "I'll get them, those darned mermaids." Mrs. Snorkel kept sighing as she looked out over the vast ocean.

And Ignatius Harkenear decided right there and then to quit his profession as an underwater detective. And he really did.

The Snorkels . . . well, I just can't be so sure.

I think they're still trying to catch mermaids. Who knows? Maybe they're just setting off again right now. . . .

HAVE MORE FIN-TASTIC FUN WITH LILLY AND FIN!

Hidden Pictures

You will find a treasure chest hidden in every picture of the main story (except for the little ones at the end of each chapter). Some are no bigger than a fingernail, so look closely. Happy treasure hunting!

If you keep your eyes peeled, you'll notice something even fishier about the illustrations in this book. Hidden in seven of the largest pictures is an animal that doesn't belong underwater. Get your goggles on, and dive with Lilly and Fin to find all seven! The answers are at the bottom of this page. No peeking!

Knit Your Own Lilly and Fin

Do you or a family member like to knit?
Check out these knitting patterns!

corneliafunke.com/en/news/knitted-underwater-heroes

Answer key: pp. 2–3 wild boar; pp. 10–11 hedgehog; pp. 28–29 lion; pp. 40–41 dog; pp. 56–57 elephant; p. 71 leopard; pp. 78–79 mouse

Lilly and Fin Game

Turn the page for a fun game you can play with Lilly and Fin!

Instructions

To begin, find a pair of dice. Then make your own two playing pieces to represent Lilly and Fin. Let your imagination swim wild, and use whatever you want! Maybe a piece of pasta or a penny. Even a paper clip could work. The world is your oyster! Remember, each player gets two game pieces.

The players take turns rolling both dice. On the first turn, move your Lilly piece the number of spaces shown on one die, and move your Fin piece the number shown on the other die. For all other turns, move the piece that is ahead the lower of the two numbers shown on the dice. Move the piece that is behind the higher number of spaces. To win the game, you have to get both of your pieces to Mermaid City, at the bottom of the board. Once one of your pieces has reached Mermaid City, you roll only one die.

Special Spaces

 STAR SPACE: The star spaces help you swim faster! When you land on a star space, you can jump to the next one.

 MORAY SPACE: Beware the hungry moray eels! If you land on one of their spaces, swim back three spaces.

 SEA DEVIL SPACE: If you land on the *Sea Devil* space, you go straight to the *Sea Devil*'s lair.

ABOUT THE AUTHOR

CORNELIA FUNKE is the *New York Times* bestselling author of many magical books for children, including *The Thief Lord, Dragon Rider,* and *Inkheart.* She was named one of the 100 most influential people by *Time* magazine in 2005. She was born in Germany and lives with her family in California.

Don't miss these funny chapter books by
CORNELIA FUNKE!

Can Tommy
teach his
monster to
behave?

Who needs a
treasure map
when you
have a pirate
pig with a
nose for gold?

Take off on a magical journey with this charming chapter book by CORNELIA FUNKE:

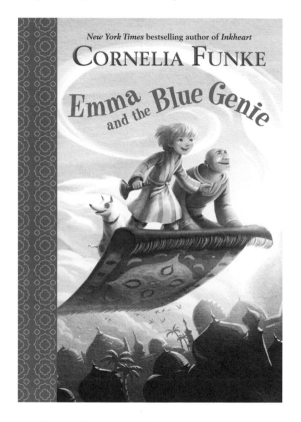

What if a genie had no wishes?
It's up to Emma and her noodle-tailed
dog to help him get his magic back!

Available now!